A STRING OF PEARL'S

Pearl Goodman had a considerable singing and acting career before turning to writing in recent years. Born and bred in Chichester, she sang to many local and national audiences before and during the last war. These included 'In Town Tonight', a season in London's Paramount Theatre and Northern Region's Children's Hour. After a five year stint in the Land Army she joined Joan Littlewood's Theatre Workshop where she acted and sang folk-songs in duo with Ewan McColl. She returned to Chichester with her husband but continued her career periodically whilst bringing up three daughters. Notably she sang soprano in Charles Grove's production of The Bartered Bride, with Wilfred Brown in The Messiah, and was 'The boy who sings on Duncton Hill' in Lord Bessborough's adaptation of Belloc's 'Four Men', which was broadcast several times. Her writing began when Ken Newbury urged her to record her memories of Somerstown for a Chichester Society social occasion. Now her evocative pieces have become widely known and she is looking forward to writing more of them. She lives with her husband David, at Halnaker, near Chichester.

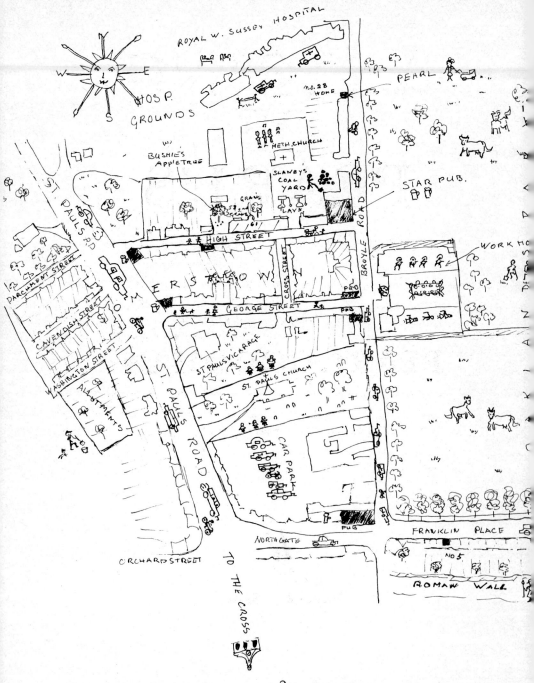

A STRING OF PEARL'S

○—○—○—○—○—○—○—○—○—○—○—○—○

PEARL GOODMAN

Illustrated by the author

Chichester · Sussex

© Pearl Goodman 1991

First published 1991 by Belfry Books
118 St. Pancras, Chichester, W.Sussex. PO19 4LV

ISBN 095183150 X

Design and typography by David Goodman

Printed by Selsey Press Ltd., 84 High Street, Selsey, W.Sussex, England

ACKNOWLEDGEMENTS

I am grateful to my family and all the kind friends who encouraged me to write this little book. I especially thank Reg Davis-Poynter who, not only first suggested the idea after reading one or two of my early pieces but, has since given essential advice and practical help in the book's production. I also record my great gratitude to my husband, who has acted throughout as editor, sub-editor, proof-reader, designer and layout artist. It was he, incidentally, who put forward the startling idea that I should draw my own illustrations. This had never even occurred to me before, so I only hope he was right! Finally I thank my dear Somerstown itself for giving me a childhood that is worth remembering.

For my brother Len

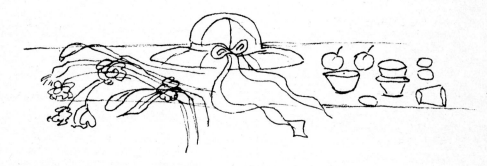

CONTENTS

FOREWORD

In the memories of my childhood I walk those sunny streets and drift and dawdle through country lanes where it is forever summer. A hand takes mine as I trail a stick from the banks of the Lavant, and whoosh!! I've hit the waters with it and my mother's blouse is covered with splashes, but I run from her, laughing. I am safe as I shall never be again.

SOMERSTOWN WITH LOVE

Somerstown, summer time, my time. This is Somerstown to me, and, like a recent bereavement, too painful to think about too often. I always thought of Somerstown as the streets I knew so well, High Street, Cross Street and George Street, but divided by the old Broyle Road there were three other streets, Parchment, Cavendish and Washington. My two sets of grandparents lived in High Street and other relations in Parchment and Cavendish, a great area to visit. I sometimes felt like the White Rabbit when I went visiting: 'Hurry, hurry, hurry, I shall be so late.'

These streets housed a few hundred people, where, as a self-conscious child, I was brought up. Self-conscious because my grandfather Wingham was a shoesmith and horse doctor at the Nag's Head, and with one other man shod all the Goodwood Estate horses. My grandfather Turner owned two taxis, ranked at the end of South Street. Most of the people in Somerstown were employed in some capacity in Chichester, but there were hard times for some, with potato picking and greening in the winter as their only jobs.

We lived next to the Hospital at the end of a row of cottages which also contained a chapel. I was an only child at that time. When I came out of my house I walked to the end of the road where the small, squat Georgian pub, the Star, stood on the corner of New Broyle Road and the High Street. High Street was unique for its many levels of dwellings. After the Star came, as my father would call it, 'the gents' lavs.', and then, two old council type cottages next door to two small red-brick ones with three steps up, an outside wall and wooden gate. I always remember a pretty woman in floral print overall, with curlers in her hair, talking to her neighbour. Next came a flint wall with a door which opened onto some waste land where stood a shack building like a garden shed. In this hovel lived an old man, a younger woman, and a child with a too-large head.

A row of pretty terraced houses in red brick were fenced and gated, with front gardens ablaze with asters and dahlias in summer. Opposite was Champion's Court, almost a ghetto for the poor and rejected, peopled only by their own kind. Next came two houses, three windows in front and two side passages, curtained with lace, and well painted. The rest of the cottages were at pavement level and very respectable. My grandmother Wingham and Mrs Matthews rejoiced in two tall houses with front gardens and snowy steps, but on the other side Mrs Fever lived in filthy squalor, always appearing at the door with coal-stained fingers, a man's cap on her head, giving that ravaged face a strange jaunty air. Next Almy Staker, legs and arms like an ox, selling cockles and whelks; gran Turner, japonica around the beetroot-red door, railings painted the same. Flint houses rubbed sides with redbrick, shacks with double fronted villas, pubs with shops and a dumping ground for old cars and ironmongery in Harding's yard. Opposite, another terrace, all painted brown or plum, and at the end, the Waggon and Horses.

Somerstown lived its own life quite separate from Chichester, a community

of which I have never known the like since. The streets were full of the constant movement of people, sitting outside, knitting, talking over the gate, or popping in and out of each other's homes like puppets, to borrow sugar, a cup of this, a cup of that . . .

It did exist. I lived there, although even writers on Chichester's history completely ignore it as though it never was.

On Sundays there was a mass exodus as the living, armed with shears and flowers, and in best clothes, with serious gait walked to the cemetery . . . I wish the singing of birds didn't always remind me of little dead Edith, uncle Tom, aunt Martha and The One Who Must Never Be Mentioned.

I turned the corner, clutching in my hand a hair ribbon and comb for my aunt to tie a butterfly bow. This alone segregated me for all time, as I had to pass Champion's Court where children, some with only dresses and no underclothes or shoes, belonged to the very poor families who lived side by side with the well fed. One did not go into the Court, but I longed to see inside and ask them what they had for their dinner - if any! When I passed they laughed and called out, and I screwed my destestable ribbon tighter in my hand, but gran Wingham's house was near and gran Turner almost next door, flanked by married daughters, as yet childless, waiting for the early morning visitor and to tie the famous butterfly bow.

High Street was the widest street, with many small Georgian cottages on both sides; Cross Street linked George Street and made it into the letter H. Opposite my grandmother's house was a small sweetshop kept by Mr Pettoe - a thin, nervous man with moustaches, who would point his toes like a ballerina and dance from cabbages to boiled sweets and, at the same time, with a deft twirl, make a cornet from paper to hold the pear drops. My

saliva runs as I remember the reds and yellows. Women stood on the handles of their brooms and chatted, doors flung open to the sun; glimpses of tables and sideboards covered with photographs of absent soldiers and sailors, crossed Union Jacks over a dead son; canary cages swinging outside, dogs yapping, rag mats rolled up and linoleum passages shining like mirrors.

Mansion Polish, Bluebell, fire smoke, cabbage cooking - I breathed it all with pleasure as I passed every house. 'Hello little Pearl - who called you that?' . . . 'How's your Mum. Lovely bow! . . .' 'I'm, alright thank you. My mum and dad had a row last night.' . . . 'You'll catch it.' . . . 'No I won't!' The women would laugh, brandishing their brooms as I walked into the dark, vinegary depths of Almy Staker's front room. 'One pot of cockles please Mrs Staker, for dad.' . . . 'Tell him not to eat them too late, duck, gives you the wind I find.' Mr Voke the baker, with horse and cart, delivered his crusty cottage loaves to every family; the muffin man rang his bell in winter, and the fish man trundled his barrow full of herrings, shouting; 'Twelve a shilling!' I thought he said 'Twelve a shittegg.'

In my grandmother Wingham's house everyone went to church. I trod the road of the righteous; church three times a day on Sunday, King's Messengers on Monday, Band of Hope on Friday, where I confessed imaginary sins because the preacher was good looking.

Vinegar belonged to one side of the road, paraffin to the other, sold by a Miss Jefferies who also sold Maynards wine gums and sherbert, which to this day have for me the flavour of paraffin. Cross Street, the linking road, had four garages. I cannot think who could have used them. In front of the garages was a wide strip of concrete. On those interminable sunny evenings I and six other girls became Broadway chorus girls. I was Billie Dove, a film actress who had short dark curly hair and a cupid's bow mouth. I was seven years old with straight fair hair and fringe. Nevertheless, when the 'Red red robin comes bob-bob-bobbing' and 'Bye bye blackbird' were sung, we high-kicked with thin legs on brocaded high heels until Fu Manchu chased us home.

On the corner of Cross Street, the only provision store, 'Mr Mant & Son', flourished, providing the streets with butter, cheese, tea, Shippams paste and bacon. We waited until April for our first taste of the luscious tomatoes, my grandmothers treat for me, with salt; and a lardy roll to mop up the vinegar. What an aroma came from that shop! The bacon slicer slicing, the smell of tea and spices, that great wall of butter and cheese to be cut into by a wire. So fascinating, so comforting . . . 'A penny lardy roll please, Mr Mant.'

George Street was where the long-bearded Jew lived his lonely life, his curtains grey, half sliding down the window, a thin, Christ- like face, topped by a skull cap. He never spoke to anyone but to himself. Whatever could his life have been? Did no-one have time for him? Large, poor families lived in George Street, with nine and ten children in two bedroomed houses. Where did they sleep?

Gentle elderly ladies in spotless curtained houses went in a band to the Mothers Union. Young wives cleaned their windows in floral overalls and waited for husbands employed by Shippams, International, the Tannery and the butchers' shops, all riding back home on their bikes. Everyone knew you: 'How's your dad, Pearlie? . . . gran alright - and your mum? . . . Lovely voice, your mum! . . . I hear you sing too, duck. Won seven and six in the fair, dint yer. 'Tired Hands', warn it? . . . Lovely song.'

My father's mother, Mrs Maria Turner, was a tough strong woman, feared by all if her mood was bad. She could fell one of her pigs with a single blow of her fist. I had four uncles, one a house decorator, one who worked at Shippams, and two who worked at the brewery. On Saturdays they would go greening and poaching, and at night sat down to rabbit stew or curry covered with white pepper, or a piece of the pig which had been so foully done to death. Chickens, pigs and donkeys abounded in the garden, hutches of ferrets lined the walls. A vine, heavy with grapes, and the loveliest lilac you ever saw, crowned this paradise for me . . . A glass of wine for a pulled tooth and a pork sandwich! . . . remembering the warning of mother to dust the chairs with my handkerchief before sitting down, as sometimes the donkeys came in. My grandmother was a formidable woman, not one to whom you could say a word out of place. I feared her as a child, but now I see her as a towering character who ruled High Street, and frightened my grandmother Wingham to death. 'Where's your other gran?' she would say. 'Still saying her prayers?' but then I loved my gentle gran Wingham, and would not answer.

When grandfather Turner was in the Crimean War times were very bad. Gran stitched soldiers' shirts for a shilling a dozen, and when expecting a child was granted by a charity fourpence a day, which she had to collect personally from the Ship Hotel, then a private house. She told me, later in life, that she had to stop and lean on window ledges and gates in the pains of labour to get her pittance. On the day she died she said to me: 'I have a lovely doctor - he's so gentle and speaks so softly. See, he brought me these

flowers.' All her life she protected the male, and now one had been a gentleman to her. I like to think she wrested from life all that was worth having. I only hope she knew it. I can hear her now: 'Don't fur me up Charles . . . I can't abide being furred up.'

The Star, the High Street pub was the centre of most activities, although there were at one time nine others in the streets. Working men crowded the little bar, drinking strong dark beer which sent them reeling home to anxious wives standing in lamp-lit doorways. 'Don't fall on me, Charlie, I'm holding a lamp!'

Every Saturday night there were darts matches and cards. My mother would sit primly in Mrs Polentine's parlour drinking her port and lemon, while I sat upon the steps outside drinking delicious draught lemonade and eating wafer thin cheese biscuits. Next to me sat Brenda Byles, a love child who lived with her mother and her mother's husband. Brenda's father was a soldier, and when he was on leave came to live with them . . . a source of great gossip when he did! There were only two bedrooms. Where did he sleep, I wondered, or where did Mr Byles sleep, or even Brenda? Patient questioning got me nowhere. But on Saturday nights, kisscurls arranged round her face, seed pearls in her ears and a band of velvet around her throat, Mrs Byles, on the arm of her husband, sat primly with my mother and sipped her stout.

Going to Chichester was referred to as 'going up town'. This was a ten minute walk from Somerstown, which I would regularly do with my Aunty Ethel and my mother, they walking in front, cotton dresses low belted, cloche hats, pink shiny stockings and patent shoes, while I pushed a superb doll's pram full of dolls, lovingly given by six aunts at various stages. I was dressed in a white crochet dress, white socks and black patent shoes, wool cape and an enormous butterfly bow; my hair a mass of frizz, having slept in rag curlers all night. I would walk well behind so I could talk to myself. My sense of perfection was so acute that I could not bear to tuck the covers in, so they were draped in a ludicrous fashion across the pram and hung down each side, catching in the wheels as I tried to push in a frenzy of temper. I would then throw out all the covers, followed by the dolls, into the road, and set up a howl.

I never failed to get both women storming back, with a hard slap on my bottom, with a further 'Wait until I get you home!' Coming back there would be ice cream at Mazzonis . . . delicious frozen custard . . . turn by 'The Bell', walk down George Street, pram still chaotic;

'What have you got there, Pearlie? Have you been crying?'

'What a naughty girl you are to your mother.'

'Got a handful there Lily!'

'Yes, she's spoiled and shows off.'

The last humiliating remark would fill me with fury. Out would come the dolls, covers after them, and the pram overturned.

'That's right, tell your gran Wingham!' as I ran to the haven, no. 61 High Street, where I could do no wrong.

'Hello, Mrs Millyard, Lily coming out?'

'No, she swallowed a button, I've just given her some castor oil.'

'I have syrup of figs or liquorice powder, but only when it is necessary!'

'Hello!" gran Wingham standing at the door.

'Come in duck, have a piece of toast and a warm.'

'Can't stay long, gran, must see gran Turner'

'Hello, gran Turner, no, I didn't kick the dog when I came in! Can't stay long. Thanks for the pickles . . . Have to see aunty Ethel, aunty Hilda, aunty Doris and aunty Vi . . . ' and they all lived in High Street!

Gathering my goodies as I went, feeling that my visit was what they were all waiting for, smelling the smells of the houses that identified them for me. Gran Wingham . . . soot and toast; gran Turner . . . pickles and dog; aunt Ethel . . . Pears soap; aunty Hilda . . . fruit cake baking; aunty Vi . . . linoleum and the smell of the kitchen.

Home at last, hope the Jellets will knock on the wall and I can go and make some more rag dolls. "Can't you ever stay in your own home?" my mother would say. But next door was full of children. Old Granfer sat by the fire, next to the copper, paraffin lamp on the table, bits of rag, and Ada to help me . . . cocoa with sugar, bread and dripping . . . knock on the wall - time to go home, clean shiny fresh home, dad playing the piano by ear . . . mum getting my comb ready, dipped in paraffin to look for non-existent nits. My mother says, if she ever finds any she will run right away. Where to? Where did she have to run to?

Oh, little girls of Somerstown, do you love and remember it as I do? Was it because I came from the largest family that I regret the passing of it so deeply?

I know I was known as 'the kid who never got dirty' — I had two clean dresses and two pairs of knickers every day. Once when I fainted in church, the scout who picked me up told his mother I was the cleanest little girl he had ever seen, and I had lace on my drawers. (He asked me to marry him, years later, but I didn't!!)

The little girls of Champion Court made me feel a privilege I never wanted. I longed to take off my shoes and socks and run bare-footed down the street. Once, in the allotments, I tried to walk on water like Jesus, and was lifted out covered with slime. I walked the whole of High Street in this state; I had never been so happy.

'You're dirty', they shouted. 'Yes', I said, 'I'm ever so dirty!' A good smacked bottom on my wet knickers soon cured my happiness . . .

When my mother used to say she would run away, I thought of the record she had about a father left with his little son, because mother had gone into the sunset, so I watched every night when the sun went down in case

24

mother went too. Next day, nevertheless, I would be dressed to perfection once more to make my visits.

Sometimes in my dreams I take this walk again. I cannot tell you about all the people of Somerstown, but they are all there in my heart, their loving faces turned towards me as, on winged feet, once more down Broyle Road, turn by The Star, meet the sunshine, run by Champion Court; 'Hello, Violet!' . . . 'Stuck up . . .' 'No I'm not', tongue out . . . Meet my young uncle Wally, aged seventeen: 'Hello, Wally' . . . 'Stuff cake up your jumper!' . . .

But gran was waiting at her door step. Tomatoes were fat and red in Mr Pettoe's shop. I would have one of those for my tea!

Now and again, when I wake in the morning, especially if it is a Sunday, I can hear again the 'Yap yap yap yap' of my gran's terrier, hunting for rabbits in the Wellington fields, the voices coming from the chapel: 'There is a happy land, far, far away.'; St Paul's bells ringing for gran Wingham to sing in her lovely Welsh voice at morning service; and, best of all, to see my young mother and father coming out of Brandy Hole Lane, my father gathering grasses, cow parsley . . . no matter what . . . to make a bouquet; and then, for Sunday night supper at gran's, to eat beef, potatoes and cold sprouts, pickles and chutney, and an apple pie made of suet crust, and gran Wingham with her high excited voice saying 'There you are, come in, my duck: Lil and Fred, Hilda and George, Doris and Bert, Ethel and Jack . . . come in!'

EMM

BEAT

EMM AND BEAT

Emily and Beatrice were known in the family as Emm and Beat. They were two of six children belonging to my aunt Nell, sister to my grandmother, and were greatly disapproved of by my mother and the rest of my aunts. They had been a source of worry to their mother when they were young; even more so when they were at last packed off to good domestic service. At twenty Emm was a bold-eyed beauty, afraid of nothing and nobody, Beat a nervous plain young woman, and a perfect foil for Emm.

When I was five years old I had tea with gran every day. My aunts, Hilda, Ethel and Doris, who were parlourmaids in the big Georgian Houses in and around Chichester, which were then fully staffed, joined us on their half days. Gran would rock with laughter at their tales of the week's events, saying "Well I never!, well I never!" over and over again.

But the names of Emm and Beat cropped up many times since those days. I remember once, when they changed their jobs three times without Aunt Nell's knowledge. On another occasion Emm asked mother if I would like to spend the week-end with them 'at their place,' General and Mrs Smiley being conveniently away. Grandad took me in his taxi to Midhurst, where I remember a large white house with many windows, surrounded by sweeping lawns, at the end of a broad drive. Over the front door a magnolia climbed, cream and luscious, and a clematis, all blue and starry fell like a cloak from a gnarled dwarf apple tree. At the back of the house, on a perfectly mown court there was a tennis net, which I enjoyed winding up and down, up and down, until I was stopped by aunty Beat banging on the window sill with a feathered brush.

I tasted every apple in the orchard, spending my first night in agony crying for my mother, but I had a lovely morning pushing my dolls pram repeatedly over white hearth-stoned steps. I was dared not to do it, but of course I did. When the cook asked me who had done it I said "nobody, I don't think!"

I must have been a rather naughty little girl. I know aunty Emm gave me a cucumber from the greenhouse to take home to my father who liked to eat it cut up with vinegar and lots of pepper, bidding me put it into my dolls pram and tell no-one, but somehow I must have taken it out and dropped it on the lawn, because later on I remember my aunt being told off by the gardener who found it, saying 'you wait, I'll tell your mother when we get home,' . . . advice I was quite used to! On the evening before I was to be taken back I was allowed to go up to General and Mrs Smileys bedroom, which was large and full of lovely polished furniture. There were what I now know to be Venetian blinds, and the evening sun made long golden bars across the white bed and blue carpet.

'Now sit still if you *can* Pearl next to Florrie the cook, and we will make you laugh.' I found it almost impossible not to pick up the delicate glass ornaments on the dressing table, and spilling the scent at the same time, just as two people came into the room. Aunty Emm had on the General's shirt, tie, trousers and jacket with a panama hat pulled down over her ears, while aunt Beat was simpering around with Mrs Smiley's garden party dress and a hat which looked like a plate of fruit. Her face was heavily rouged, while Emm had painted a moustache on her own top lip. Florrie and I laughed so much that we did not hear the motor car draw up. Suddenly the front door opened and I heard a voice say 'Emily, Beatrice, come and help with the luggage.'

I don't know what happened after that; everyone seemed to be pushing me and I heard aunt Beat say 'The old womans back.' That evening my grandfather came for me in his taxi and I heard voices saying 'disgraceful, how dare you, take a months notice,' and 'who is that child?' . . . 'Yes we will, and be glad to go, won't we Beat?' shouted Emm . . . 'Yes Emm' said Beat. My Grandfather was standing at the back door in the peaked hat he wore when he drove his taxi. 'Come on my duck' he said winking his eye. 'I'll be back for you Emm and Beat, when you let me know. . . . are they in trouble again? 'Yes' I said 'they are in very great trouble again.' I remember Emm still in the General's clothes, and streaky tears running down Beat's ludicrous cheeks. Mrs Smiley, who was a large lady with a red face, glared at me, but I said what I thought was polite. 'Thank you, Mrs Smiley for having me,' because I had had a very good time.

My Mother said I was not to go and stay with them *ever* again, but I knew I couldn't wait till next time!

GOING TO THE PICTURES

Friday was always the night mum and aunty Ethel went to the pictures and this they continued to do for the rest of their active lives. I was often invited to come too, as a treat, which indeed it was.

One evening, at Northgate walking between the two women, I saw aunty Vi and uncle Alf drive their motor bike up on the other side of the road where there was a small pub next to a group of Georgian cottages and a blacksmiths, all enclosed within a courtyard. There too was a pretty double-fronted cottage with an exquisite garden where tulips were in full flower. It belonged to a distant relative of ours, a Mr and Mrs Kimball who owned the pork butchers shop in East Street.

On the outside wall of the pub was a wrinkled poster in blue and red advertising *Rio Rita*, and starring Bebe Daniels. We stopped and waved to aunty Vi, 'but she called out 'I'm coming over'. She was a very pretty woman and quite the most fashionable aunt I had. This day she was wearing a sleeveless summer dress covered in poppies. She had on pink silk stockings with high heeled black patent shoes. 'It's a drama Lily' she said 'It's lovely, take a handkerchief'.

A cloud of California Poppy floated back as she nipped on to the back of the bike. 'We are going to *Rio Rita* on Saturday. If you bring Pearl I'll bring Queenie' 'Oh good,' I said. Queenie, my cousin was an old conspirator, and we knew how to ruin everyone's evening. One more wave and with a loud bang the motor bike jerked forward. 'I don't know how she can,' said Ethel, pressing her lips together, 'It's not ladylike'. But dad approved of aunty Vi. 'If more women rode motor bikes' he said 'they wouldn't have so many headaches.' I could never understand this.

I was allowed Maynards Wine Gums for the pictures since they were supposed not to hurt teeth, and these we bought in Mickey's shop, then situated by the alley, and Carpenter's fish and chip shop in North Street. Further down, in the house which is now The Ship Hotel lived Dr Scase. One of my mother's friends, named Miss Lemon, was housekeeper there and I often stayed weekends with her. Lady Turing's large white painted Georgian house stood imposingly on the opposite side of the street, where a parlour maid, in a coffee coloured apron opened the door to morning callers. Not far up on the same side stood Arthur Purchase's wine shop. It was small and select and provided the wine for the well-to-do of the city.

I used to get very irritated by my mother and aunt who walked very very slowly, talking all the time, so I hopped in between the paving stones carefully avoiding the cracks!

By seven o'clock we had arrived at the Corn Exchange and bought our tickets; fourpence for children, sevenpence for adults and if you were very well off, one shilling and ninepence. As soon as the swing-doors closed behind me I entered a new world, redolent with scented air and orange peel. Sometimes my mother and aunt were so busy talking and finding their seats that they quite forgot about me, so I would find myself in a

32

different row.

I know I was transfixed as though in a dream, watching the hero and heroine, the latter in a silk sleeveless dress with a string of pearls around her throat, while the handsome hero, black hair slicked back with a small moustache, passionately bent her back and kissed her cupid bow lips. All conversations were printed on a black screen between scenes but generally all I could read was *Kiss* or *Love* before it was replaced by the next torrid scene. 'The Pictures' I'm sure, contributed significantly to my romantic idea of the life I thought was before me!

When the picture came to an end there was always a long interval when raffle tickets were sold, and if you were lucky you might win dinner plates or silk stockings. Not that mum ever indulged in such things of course!

Scented sprays were puffed out of cylinders by usherettes who wore shiny black and white dresses and huge red bows on their shingled heads. A lady who looked like a man and shouted *Chocolates and Cigarettes* was known as "Old Chocolates" in the town. I know I tried to get a glimpse of her legs just in case she was wearing trousers, and I can remember being pulled up from the floor, (which was always covered in monkey nut shells) by mum who turned to my aunt and said 'Look at her, you bring them up —- stand still!' At this point she brought out a handkerchief with which to rub my face and I said very loudly 'don't spit on it.'

The lights went down again and we saw a cowboy film with Tom Mix or Rin Tin Tin the wonder dog. I never sat on my seat but stood up leaning on the seat in front, sucking my wine gums. Once I got told off by a lady with a large hat who told me to stop chewing in her ear and turning to my mother with 'Can't you stop talking and look after your child?' 'Cheek' said mum giving me a slap. 'Do you know Lily,' said Ethel, 'they are thinking of making the actors talk. It would never take on. They say they sound like parrots.'

On and on they used to go, until once a whole row turned round to say, *Shhh!* in unison. My face went hot. 'That's why I don't go with them' said dad, cycling for once without guilt for his pint.

The magic of the evening over I once more walked behind the two women who sauntered slowly through the lighted streets, the shops still open, while they continued their everlasting conversations. Dreamy-eyed and unseeing I remained locked in the drama of the last film, carefully putting the last wine gum into my mouth and wondering how I could get to Hollywood.

MUSHROOMING

A milky white dawn and the Wellington fields are full of mushrooms. I ride on the carrier of dad's bike and we meet uncle Alf and aunty Vi who have just arrived on an old motor bike. Uncle Bill and Sid drag their feet along the road as they bring their brakeless boneshakers to a halt.

No one talks as they gather their bags and baskets and make for the fields. I take my small basket; the grass, is wet with dew and so are my socks. 'Dad' I say 'Is this a mushroom?' I show him broken pieces of fungus. 'All you have to do' he says 'is smell them, but show every one to me.'

I watch the five industrious mushroom pickers and feel very cold. Carefully I sit down on the grass, take my shoes and socks off and put them in the basket. I stand up, my dress is wet too, but the feel of the damp earth on my curling toes reminds me of Bognor. I look back at the basket with the shoes and socks inside and the broken bits of mushroom. Perhaps gran would like them. Aunty Vi comes back and looks at me, 'Fred, Fred' she says 'Just come and look at her, she's wet through. What ever will Lily say?'

Dad comes back with a large basket of mushrooms. I look at him: 'dad' I say, 'I don't think I shall come again'. He takes off his scarf and tries to dry me down. 'No,' he says, 'I don't think so either when your mother sees this.' He lights up a Woodbine.

But the sun is up now and the cows are straggling out of the cowsheds. A man with a stick urges them into another field. How they stand and stare! I pick six blackberries to take home to my mother. We all start back. The motor bike is cranked up and aunt Vi sits astride behind uncle Alf and shows a piece of lace on her drawers. Off they go. 'See you at the "Star" Fred. 'Love to Lily' calls Vi with a wave and a cloud of blue smoke. Dad and I ride back behind Bill and Sid. They raise their arms in farewell as we pass them.

Turning left at the "Star", dad dismounts at our house and mum opens the door. I know she is cross when she sees me so I uncurl my fingers and offer a handful of purple mush. 'Thank you,' she says, and gives me a kiss. 'Can I go again next week?' I say, smiling up at her.

NOVEMBER

Shafts of rosy evening light
Slide down on rick and roof
And softly tip the rabbits ear
And gild the pheasant's tail

The fragrant orbs of goblin quince
Glow gold in orchard grass
And through the branches drifts
A leaf, an apple falls, the last.

GOING TO PORTSMOUTH

One day dad decided to take out a rowing boat in Portsmouth Harbour, so with great excitement we scrambled in, including a disapproving mother.

'Now sit down Lily' he said 'and just pretend you are on holiday'. Mum became very offended, but he knew he always made us laugh when he teased her.

Thinking we had rowed out far enough she said, 'take me back Fred or I shall get out,' 'You do that my girl' he said. We watched, knowing full well what the outcome would be. She actually stood up as though to get out, but sat down quickly assuring dad that 'It was the last time she would go anywhere with him'. What a lovely woman you are to take on holiday', he bitterly replied as she sat bolt upright staring at the dimming shore. What dad would have done without mum as a butt for his humour, I do not know!

Sit doww Lily!

THIS AND THAT

Mum was famous for her sayings like, 'waltzing up to the grocers' and 'dragging myself down to the doctors.' She never scorched a shirt but 'swealed it'. A day's cleaning was 'firking' out all the dirt. When the joint was cut, the juice from it was called 'jipper'.

People my father disliked were called 'bolshie,' and if they didn't understand what he was talking about they were a lot of 'dinloes'. Be rude to dad and they needed to be 'chinned' and if they interrupted him, 'putting their vardi in'. When things were right they 'ackled', when he felt hungry quite 'lear', and when everything went totally wrong 'a complete washout'.

SHIPPAMS CONCERT

Every year just before Christmas, Shippams factory, one of the major industries of Chichester which employed about two hundred men including my father, gave a concert by any volunteers who could perform.

Dad had a very lyrical tenor voice, contributing at least two songs and organising the young cutter boys. These were the boys who stood by the men at the filler machines and neatly cut the tops off the paste from the jars before the lids were stamped on. Their ages ranged from fourteen to twenty or thereabouts.

The year of my 12th birthday dad decided to put on a little musical of his own called "The Wedding of the Painted Doll". About a month before the concert, the cutter boys began rehearsing once a week at our house. The sitting room was given a thorough turning out and the rosewood piano with its decorated fretwork silk front was shifted to get a better tone and the fire was lit in the small grate.

Before the boys arrived, dad in his best suit (the one he was married in) sat down on the revolving stool and played the first song by ear. Meanwhile, I ran upstairs and tried to do my hair in a different style. I could not possibly

be seen in my hateful school uniform, so I changed into the one best dress I owned, slapped my cheeks and bit my lips to make them redder. I was then ready to open the door to the first well scrubbed young man who arived. I was not allowed into the room but was made to do my homework. 'What on earth have you changed your clothes for?, and for goodness sake do your hair properly', my mother said.

Meanwhile, sandwiches made from Shippams Bloater Paste and cups of Camp Coffee were taken in by me. I shut the kitchen door hastily in case the noise my brother and sister made could be heard by the young men, for I did not want them to think that I belonged to that domestic scene.

But when I had handed the sandwiches round with a coy smile, dad firmly told me to 'Go and help your mother' Then his voice sweet and true led all the young tenors. My mother joined in the singing while she washed up. In another age the quality of her rich mezzo-soprano voice, together with my fathers tenor could have made them professional singers. We three children inherited their talent.

At last the night arrived, dad trying out his voice at every opportunity and sucking throat sweets galore. 'You are not going to break down are you Fred?', enquired mum anxiously. 'Listen to her' said dad, 'If I see your mother's and her sister's faces in the audience, it will put me right off!'

I well remember the night I sat with mum and aunty Ethel in the audience at the Assembly Rooms. They never stopped talking, their conversation always following the same pattern. 'Well Ethel, why should you'. 'Lily I'm not going to, every one takes you for granted and I've had enough of it'. 'So have I Ethel'. 'What does Pearl want for Christmas?' 'Give her a vest Ethel' A vest, I thought bitterly.

Suddenly the lights went down. 'I do hope he doesn't forget his words Ethel' said mum. Joe Marsh sat down at the piano and a chorus of young men dressed as flappers came on with a Broadway Chorus Act. It was hard to believe they were not girls with their rouged cheeks and their red pouting lips.

Meanwhile Dad performed a high kicking dance on the right side of the stage. When the magician called for a helper I was up there before anyone could stop me. I could understand what dad meant about my mum's face, which I too always tried to avoid looking at. Then Bert Wheeler came on to sing "Susannah," a favourite tune, and "Old Macdonald had a Farm" complete with smock and straw hat, finally ending the act by announcing that he would whistle with a cigarette in his mouth. How an unlit Woodbine dangling from his lips added to his performance one might well ask.

A stand-up comic came next and mum whispered to auntie Ethel 'He was a bit much'. Finally dad sang "Charmaine". He did not break down and brought the loudest applause of the evening.

All this was my father at his best. He was far too intelligent for his menial jobs, feeling frustrated and angry most of the time. He had left the West Sussex Regiment as an Acting Sergeant Major when he was only twenty-five. During his eight years service, all of it in India and Mesopotamia, he showed a great deal of courage and mental fortitude. He really should have gone back to India after the war, but mum would not go with him, so he had to be content with jobs which were beneath his capabilities. Nevertheless, he was so determined that his children should be well read, that he put by sixpence a week from his meagre two and sixpence pocket money to buy us the classics, all on offer from the Daily Herald. He introduced me to the kind of reading which few girls in my circle at that time enjoyed.

His knowledge of politics was considerable and as a member of the Labour Party, he held a little meeting in the house every week with a few dedicated men who tried to make the lives of their families and fellow workers a little better.

The concert over, with many congratulations all round, dad flushed with pleasure, and relieved by success, mounted his bike and was away to have his pint at the "Star", leaving mum her sister and me disconsolately outside the Assembly Rooms! My mother's friends did not approve of their husbands drinking, so they had to make do with home-made wine. Men under such marital control were called "Ninnies" by dad. 'I might just as well be a widow, in fact some people think I am!' mum said to dad. 'Indeed Lily' he replied, 'indeed; and which lovely friend of yours said that? Not dear Maude surely, not with that husband she has, not even allowed to buy his own shag?'. They had nothing in common with each other and had no illusions about that!

'What's the name of your cutter boy dad?' I said, 'cause he smiled at me.' 'Did he my duck?', answered dad, winking at me: 'Don't tell your mother'. Mum was a great butt for my dad's teasing. It was as if he were trying to say, 'Come and join me Lily in the real world,' but her world was not his nor mine, and she was just as entitled to her own! What he could not bear was having to live according to what the neighbours thought, yet this took up a great deal of my mother's life. Whenever there was an argument (and there were plenty) she immediately closed the windows, whereupon he opened them again. Nevertheless mum gave us all spiritual values and was intensely interested in what we did. She liked nothing better than to listen to my stories or recount what was going on in the family of her sisters, relating their conversations to her own. The house was fresh and spotless, with flowers everywhere, although I never saw her tend the garden or pluck a weed! Everyday throughout her married life she washed and changed at four o'clock so that we were always greeted by a neat pretty mother when we came home from school. Sometimes she looked worried and strained, especially if a chore had not be completed, but once done, her lovely singing voice resounded throughout the house and dad would put his Daily Herald down and look very moved. But he still could not resist saying 'Can't she ever get the words right?'

I once bought her some daffodils and as I stood in the sunlit room and offered them to her, she said years later that she would always remember me that way. I think my mother was a closer companion to my sister Jean than to me, whereas dad was closer to his son Len. I was given a rather different kind of loving as the daughter who sang and acted, telling exciting stories which gave them a little of the reflected glory they had never experienced themselves at first hand. That was my kind of loving.

45

AUNTY ETHEL'S WEDDING

When my aunts were courting I was allowed to go with them, trailing behind each couple who had to suffer me, and picking my own bouquet from the hedgerows. It puzzled me why two of the young men wore shoes and the other one boots. I felt very sorry for my uncle Bert, who wore the boots, as I thought he must be very poor. Aunty Ethel and uncle Fred walked arm in arm and I walked behind, sometimes picking up a stick or small stone to throw at their unheeding backs. I used to wonder how one found a young man, and when I asked one of my young uncles he would say, 'Oh, you just wink at them!'

I took this seriously, so whenever we passed young men in Brandy Hole Lane I made a grotesque face, while they gave me a pitying look, for of course I would be then about six or seven years old. What lovely walks they were, usually on a Sunday afternoon, with sun-dappled lanes where wild borders of cow parsley grew, old man's beard, and deadly nightshade. Gran said: 'If you so much as touch it, you die directly.'

When I got tired I was lifted upon my uncle's shoulders to see the white-gold fields of corn, and grazing cattle in the panorama of lovely Sussex. Sometimes, when I followed my other aunts and uncles, watching them as they too walked arm in arm, I would pick grasses and flowers and listen to the murmuring couple who laughed and then looked at each other. It seemed a strange thing, this courting . . . I did not like it because no-one had any time for me, and invariably when we came home my aunt would say: 'It's the last time we are taking Pearl!'

After many of these walks I was told by my mother one evening, I would soon have to tie my own bow, as aunty Ethel was getting married and I was to be a bridesmaid. It seemed as though aunty Ethel became someone quite different. I was completely overwhelmed by my excited adults. 'Go and sit on that chair, Pearl, and don't move — here's a ball.' I ask you . . . ! Or standing for what seemed hours while materials were pinned on to me by aunty Doris and aunty Hilda, their mouths made grim by holding too many pins in them, until I cried with tiredness. No more petting, nor swinging on young uncle's arm — just 'run and play . . . run and play . . . .'

Aunty Ethel looked like the Virgin Mary to me, with white satin draped from shoulder to toe, and some beautiful gauzy stuff with little white flowers on each side of her head. Oh how lovely she looked, just how I must look one day. I would soon wink at somebody and I too would become a Virgin Mary with a nice uncle to marry.

My three aunts were in domestic service in Chichester, one a cook and the other two parlourmaids. They worked in some of the loveliest Georgian houses in the city. Sometimes I was allowed to visit one of my aunts and while they disappeared into the magnificence of the front of the house I tried to catch a glimpse of the family sitting at table. So much silver and glass, cigar smoke, red wine and food I had never seen before, but there was always a little for me when it came to the kitchen. I could not believe that all this trouble was to be taken to serve a few people for dinner. At least eight servants were helping to prepare one meal.

When it was over at last, I was allowed to enter the smoky Aladdin's cave and be enraptured by the lovely cigar-scented rooms, velvet curtains, soft to the touch, and lace tablecloths draped to the floor; oil paintings of horses and hunting; wonderful displays of flowers, and best of all, a great dish of fruit, piled high, and another of black grapes. I don't know why they impressed me so much. Perhaps they symbolised all the luxury I had ever seen, but there were always massive dishes of fruit which must have cost a fortune to a little girl who had one penny a week to spend.

One evening the lady of the house came into the kitchen and said: "And who is this little girl?
I said, 'My name is Pearl', and she replied, 'I think Pearl is a lovely name and you can choose yourself an apple.'
But I knew my father loved cucumbers so I asked: 'Could I have a cucumber instead?'
Of course the inevitable happened. My aunt said "It's the last time Pearl is taken there!"

But Mrs Blaker did laugh, and didn't mind a bit. I didn't see why she should, with all that fruit . . .

But now all my aunts were home at my grandmother's for their day off, to prepare for the wedding. Presents arrived and stood in gran's parlour. Glasses and cake dishes, cup and saucers, vases, peppers and salts, cake tins . . . Then one by one the neighbours came in to throw up their arms and exclaim: 'Don't they make things nice now — different in our day, eh Kate?'

Aunty Hilda made a beautiful cake, covered in white icing — a bit like aunty Ethel, I thought. Granny Wingham with her high excited voice, called: 'Lil, don't forget you promised a sponge! . . . Where's that young Wally? . . . '
'Out of the way from all of *you*!' he shouted back.
My uncle Wally was only seventeen, so that whenever he passed me he would push me and say, 'Go and tell your gran,' or 'Stuff cake up your jumper.' Once he took me up the garden and told me to look under the gooseberry bush, where I would find something nasty like myself. Then he gave me such a push that I went sprawling under the rhubarb.

I often wonder if it was from my young uncle that I acquired my fascination for difficult sarcastic men . . . Even when I was grown up he would say the rudest things to me, . . . but he was very handsome!
'Put your nose out of joint has it, Pearlie?' he would say, since no-one seemed to have any time for me.

My aunts and granny sat around the fire making the bridesmaids' dresses, while I, with two enormous knitting needles and a ball of grubby wool, cast on ten stitches, dropped five, and threw the rest in the fire.
'Oh, you . . . you . . . spoiled ----'
With every word I got a cuff from each one, but gran said, 'Leave her alone, those rings on your fingers hurt her little head. Have some toast darling.' This, I insisted, was buttered on the browner side, and not the hotter.

Large bunches of flowers were brought to the house to decorate the church. Material was scattered everywhere; scissors sliced away and machines whirred; tins of cakes and goodies were left in the house by neighbours and friends, and I became so excited, especially when my dress went over my head and everyone said 'Pearl's a princess — Pearl's a queen!' Then I would become slightly mollified, finally to be dragged home by my mother for the great day.

There was only one thing that marred the wedding day for me. Mum had a guard that stood around the fire, and I was very used to leaning on it to warm my legs. My bridesmaid's dress was plum velvet, with a lace collar, and on my head a lace cap. While I waited for everyone to get ready, I stood in my old place, leaning on the fireguard. Of course the entire criss-cross pattern of it came off on my dress!

Mum was called down from dressing, and only my lace cap saved me from having a box round the ears. Off came the dress, and boiling steam from the kettle was applied to it. But until the day when it was finally torn up for dusters, the criss-cross remained.

The greatest luxury for me was the ride in grandad's taxi to the church and then back to gran's for the wedding feast. A clean starched cloth was put on the large kitchen table, and upon this Trimalchio's feast the wedding cake rose up like a white pagoda I once saw in a book. Pork brawn, in fancy moulds, slices of rose-pink ham, curling like many tongues, piled on dishes; lettuce from the garden; bunches of watercress which gran said had been through six washes!
'I'm funny about watercress', she used to say, 'Your poor aunt Flossie was taken so bad once.'
'I don't know about your sponge . . . Lil never was much good at cakes, were you?'

Much to my mum's mortification, my grandmother had something to say about everything that had been contributed.

My chewing was punctuated by kicks under the table from Uncle Wally, and kicks back from me, until my grandfather banged on the table with his fork. A glass of port was then handed round with a slice of cake, the icing of which I gave to the dog. The last bit of wobbly jelly slid down my throat and the rest slid down my dress.

After the meal we all strolled into gran's pretty garden, dominated by a large apple tree bearing little rosy apples which everyone had for Christmas. My aunt was still in her wedding dress, and neighbours came out in their gardens to wish the couple happiness. I remember one said 'Come on, Pearl give us a song,' so I stood on the wood chopper and sang 'He's My Dark-eyed Sailor', which gran had taught me.
'You ought to go on the stage?'
'Put her on the stage, Lil!'
They little knew that this was just where I *was* going . . .

Pretty aunty Ethel, in her white satin and pearls, with her gentle husband; evening sunshine touching the hair and clothes of my other young aunts; uncles in their best suits, leaning against the apple tree, their cigarette smoke curling up towards the branches; my mother, father and loving grandmother, and my own life before me. I shall never forget that day.

Everyone I loved was in the cottage garden. Mr Jenner sang "The Laughing Policeman"; my father sang "Love's Old Sweet Song".
'Getting a bit chilly isn't it, Lil', dad said — a sure sign that he wanted to "wet his whistle". Into the house and through to the front parlour for sherry, port and beer, and a glass of wine for me.

'Go and see your gran Turner,' mum said, 'and show her your dress'
I knew only too well what the reception would be there!
'Oh, you've come at last, have you? . . . Not even a piece of cake!'
'I'll get you some, gran'
'No thanks . . . don't like cake I haven't made myself . . . Gives me heart-
burn. Who made your dress? . . . Are those marks *supposed* to be on the
back? . . . Your gran Wingham was done up, wasn't she? . . . I see Emm and
Beat had to poke their noses in . . .'

'Gran, you were asked to come', I said fearfully. Then her voice became
kind, and she said, 'I know I was, duck, but I just can't be tuckered up with it
— go and get yourself a bunch of grapes off the wall' (an abundant vine
clung there.) 'Give my best wishes to Ethel and Fred . . . I suppose you
think you are going to marry a lord, don't you, Pearlie?'
'Yes, if he is good looking, gran'
'You mind — men are all the same! I ought to know'
She should indeed, with six sons and a husband grown childish, with an
incurable disease.

Half frightened, half admiring, I stood and looked into her face. The
protector of the male, the pioneer woman — kill for her children — that was
my grandmother Turner.
'I don't know, Pearl', she would say, 'it's a funny old world!'
'Have you enjoyed your life, gran?'
'Let's say I've had my moments! Well, run along in or your gran Wingham
will be fussing about and calling you.'

Not reluctantly I went off, saddened by her hard life. But my spirits lifted
when I entered the darkened passage leading to the kitchen, and then into
the twilit garden of the wedding party. Gran, aunt Martha and aunt Nell,

looking like a coven of witches - white hair springing from broad brows, dark skirts and blouses, jet beads and brooches winking in the darkening garden every time a pipe was lit.

They had all lost one child, I knew, because of the Sunday visits to cut the grass round the little mounds in the cemetery. Sometimes I used to look at the faded sepia photographs of long-dead children and wonder if they had ever been flesh and blood, but were only images.

Dad at this time had always 'had about enough'. Nothing stopped him from going for his pint at nine o'clock at The Star. Mum was always ashamed of this, since no other man would want, or be allowed, to go. But I liked to go, and after a hasty goodbye to everyone, and a special one for gran, I took my dad's arm and skipped my way to the next excitement: cheese and biscuits and draught lemonade, sitting on the steps of the pub in my bridemaid's dress, and causing quite a stir.

RACE WEEK

On race week my mother let the front bedroom to a Mr and Mrs Roberts who came down from London in a taxi. He was a large man with a very red face and shiny black hair, dressed in a dark suit with white collar and a silk tie with a gold pin in it. Madge Roberts was a handsome bosomy lady who usually wore a dress with a jacket, large hat and pearls around her throat. Race people always wore pearls, or so it seemed to me.

On the same day Prince Monolulu, a splendid figure in richly embroidered tribal costume, his noble mahogany face topped by turban and waving ostrich feathers, strode down the sunny High Street of Somerstown shouting 'I gotta horse I gotta horse' like some exotic pied piper.

A crowd of excited children followed his sandaled heels until he reached his lodging at number twenty, a little palace, respectable and clean. It was the only palace he was likely to know.

The week before the Roberts were expected, the whole house was put through a late Spring Clean. Dad was instructed to colour wash the outside lavatory and do the innumerable other painting jobs, while mum washed and starched like boards, polished her shining floors and shone the "brights".

Going to the Trundle

MRS JELLET

ADA

SUZI

Dad said it was all unbearable. He would like to be 'rubbed right out', until the Roberts left. When the taxi pulled up outside number five Franklin Place, the neighbours were agog. Mum stood by the open gate, neatly dressed. 'Ready to curtsey' said dad.

We children had to have our tea early so that mum could cook dinner for her guests, usually a roast joint, accompanied by runner beans, peas and

carrots, grown by dad in our garden. Mum had a special dinner service for visitors. This was in the inevitable willow pattern, and I can vividly see the bright blue plates on the smooth, white, starched linen cloth, well laid with Sheffield plate forks and sharp steel knives, all cleaned with brown powder every Saturday by me!

In the centre of the table were the flowers which were always in the house.

Dad never hurried although he knew mum wanted everything ready by the time the Roberts had washed and changed in the bedroom, but strolled around with a towel tucked into the neck of his shirt and shaving soap still on his face. 'I'll tell you what I would like to be doing,' he said on one occasion 'just sitting in the garden, dead to the world. They are not royalty, you know Lily.' Now all this was quite exciting, especially since a list of runners was given to dad, who then took it to the "Star" for his mates to place bets. These were then given to our Mr Roberts, who was a bookie.

As the Roberts slept in my parent's room they, (mum and dad), were in mine, and my little sister and brother were in the end bedroom. This meant that I had to sleep with Miss Morton, a lady with a cork leg. Our home was cheerful and brightly lit, but Miss Morton's was dark and depressing. The whole house smelled of paraffin, for she still used oil lamps.

At nine o'clock I reluctantly left home, where the Roberts were opening bottles of beer and taking out the cards, to go to my lodgings down the road. When I knocked at the door I could hear Miss Morton's cork leg banging down the passage, the paraffin smell overpowering. I was given a candle and told to go to bed.

Bamboo-framed quotations from the bible hung on every wall. After saying my prayers I climbed into a large lumpy feather bed where, thank goodness, I soon fell asleep, only to be wakened by Miss Morton unstrapping her leg and standing it against the wall while I, terrified, recited a poem until it was all over.

I only had one other choice and that was to sleep with my gran, who would not open the window and could not sleep until every moth was slapped to death with her petticoat. This could take a long time and was very noisy.

Finally the day came for the departure of the Roberts. We all lined up to say good-bye and received a half crown pressed into our willing palms.

'Such nice people', my mother said. 'Yes,' replied dad: 'Pity his tips came nowhere, I felt a right charlie up at the 'Star',' Nothing could have pleased my mum more than to hear this. I am sure she was planning to buy another strip of coconut matting with a red border, to lay down in the kitchen.

The week had been worth it for her at least and I thankfully fell asleep in my own bed not having to recite, "Oh, to be in England now that April's here."

A DAY IN THE COUNTRY

Every summer my grandmother visited her relations the Wilkins in Donnington, a village about four miles from Chichester, and I always accompanied her. Sharp at nine o'clock I left 26 Broyle Road in my best sprigged cotton dress, with knickers to match. My frizzed hair had now disappeared, and I had a neat bob with a fringe, cut for sixpence by a cousin who was learning the trade. It took an hour and a half to do it, but Oh My! I did feel something in my new dress especially as it was sleeveless!

To show this off I wore my cardigan pulled down around my elbows. I can't think who could have been interested. In fact, to my absolute mortification, a friend of my mother's said, 'What hairy arms Pearl has. And just look at her legs. Good job she's fair. Still, it means she's strong, Lily.'

'Are you ready, duck?' gran asked as I opened the door of 61 High Street, and smelled the old familiar smell of Mansion Polish and cats' fish, boiling on the fire. 'Yes, I'm ready gran; and mum says I'm to wipe the seats of the chairs before I sit down, with this handkerchief.'

'Yes, I would if I were you, they're none too particular in the country, but it's clean dirt, that's what I say.'

Gran covered my grandfather's dinner with a plate, damped down the fire, covered the milk with the piece of muslin with four beads on it which I had lovingly made at school, and finally put out the cat, only to go round it all once again to see if she had forgotten anything. At last it was time for her to change into her smart herring-bone tweed suit, black stockings and button shoes, skewer her hat firmly on her white, unruly hair with her pearl-topped hat-pin, draw on her cotton gloves - and we were ready.

All this time I watched the weather anxiously. If it rained before we were about to set off, then we didn't go . . . But once started I didn't care if there was a typhoon, because at least that meant we would have to keep going.

As we passed through the streets of Somerstown, trying to avoid the dust from the rag mats being dashed against the walls and fences, neighbours stopped sweeping their pavements to say "Have a nice day, Mrs Wingham and little Pearl." Always when we reached Mazzoni's ice cream shop I was filled with trepidation. I knew what my grandmother would say: 'Pearl, my duck, run back and see if I have locked the door and put the key under the mat, will you?'
'But gran', I wailed, 'I saw you!'
'Never mind; just run back and see.'
When I had turned the corner I kicked the wall in a paddy. I wouldn't have done such an errand for anyone else, that's for sure!

Once on the Selsey Road, gran strode rather than walked, holding down her hat. We fairly ran, like the Duchess and Alice in Wonderland. 'Come on Pearl, keep up if you want to make old bones,' she said over her shoulder, as I lagged behind. When we came to some gabled cottages she slowed down, looked searchingly at them, and said, 'That's where I was born; let me see, Charlie and Tom slept in that room, and we girls all in one bed in the front. Oh the times we had. My mother used to send us to pick up the milk from the farm, but I would throw the milk can at my brother and run across the fields, over the stile and gates, to pick bulrushes and make a bouquet; but when I had finished making them, anyone could have them . . . I never wanted to bring them home.'

She recounted this little story as though she couldn't quite understand her own actions. 'You'd think I would have brought them to my mother - but there!' and she became quiet, looking back and remembering the flying red haired figure. Soon she stopped again and said 'That's the school I used to teach in.' 'And where did you meet grandad, gran?' 'Never you mind. You want to know too much, young Pearl.' And I knew that was all I would get about her private life.

On and on we went, I picking wild flowers and trying to keep up, but gran showing no signs of fatigue. At last we turned into the lane where aunt Kate and uncle George lived, next door to their son and his wife. The lane was bordered by hedgerows and thick with nettles and deadly nightshade. 'If you touch that you'll die directly,' was the ominous warning.

Soon we came to a clearing where the gabled cottage stood. Aunt Kate with her red cheeks, snowy hair and faded blue blouse and skirt waited at the gate.
'Our Rene,' she called: 'aunt Alice and Pearl are here!'

The gate always made the same scroopy sound as you pushed it open, and then we were in the garden, a riot of scent and colour.
There was a dog on a long chain, nearly demented with excitement, two mother cats with three kittens, and the face of the old horse who had come across the field to push its head forward for stroking, and auntie's canary

singing its heart out in its cage, hooked up in the apple tree. What a day lay before me! 'Oh, let it last longer than most days please, please God!' This was said very quietly, as you only mentioned God in church, according to gran.

When we walked into aunt Kate's kitchen it smelled to me of a mixture of earth and cold water. A fire burned even in summer, for there was no other way to cook in those days. The parlour was stuffed with furniture and there were three antimacassars on every chair. Since the family never sat in there I wondered from whose heads they were protected. We were given clear home-made orange wine, although gran always tipped half of mine back.

Gran and aunty exchanged news by shouting it to one another, although their faces were only inches apart. If I sat patiently I could then ask if the wax Victorian lady, kept in a glass case, could be wound up. When this was done she slowly raised her lorgnettes to her eyes and down again, accompanied by a tune played by a musical box.

'Now Pearl,' said aunt Kate, 'Go and find Rene.' Rene was her granddaughter, a beautiful, brown, long legged girl of fifteen, who did everything a boy could do. She rode the horses bare-backed, climbed the walnut tree, slid down the highest rick and always wore short trousers.

Oh, the envy I felt at such freedom. Alas! her freedom came to an end, for she died still a young woman, but her image remained with me for years. Just to wander across the fields and listen to Rene tell me about her boy-friends was a delight. It was a world I had not yet entered, but I was more than willing to hear of the treats in store. We came across her lovesick swain throwing stones into the pond and pretending we were not there. He, with slightly heightened colour, and making figure eights with his shoe in the dust, said finally, 'Are you going up to Chichester Saturday night, Rene?' 'I might' said Rene. 'Meet you in Woolworth's?' 'You might' said Rene. 'All right, see you there,' he replied, as he kicked a stone skilfully, and with not one glance at me, was off on his bike.

'Do you go out with him?'

'Yes.' said Rene, 'but not actually go out. My gran wouldn't like it. He's alright, anyway. I don't care if I do or I don't!'

'Coo,' I thought admiringly, 'I would.'

I didn't think I would tell *my* gran. She always said, very severely, 'Enough time for that sort of thing later on.' But there had not been much time left for Rene. I can see her now, running beside her horse, holding on to the mane. Over would go her flying legs, to straddle the galloping mare, red hair flying, her brown face looking at me over her shoulder.

No such thoughts clouded my brow that brilliant afternoon, as we all sat round the large table for dinner. On the starched white cloth was cold mutton, and boiled potatoes, followed by a cornflower blancmange. A simple meal enjoyed by uncles George, Charlie and Tom.

All my uncles were politically minded. Uncle George was known as Lloyd George, because of his marvellous oratory. When they talked together they all shouted at one another. One of the uncles, a quiet man, was an old bachelor, and my mother told me that when she was expecting my brother, she was told to sit down and put the corner of the tablecloth over her lap. 'Then uncle Tom wouldn't notice, as 'he didn't know anything about that sort of thing.'

In fact he had never walked out with a girl - well, not as aunt Kate could remember. "Good Lor'," exclaimed gran.

All the men worked on the farm. When they had retied their gaiters they took up their scythes and still arguing in their lovely Sussex accents, went back to the fields, with: 'And don't you be late with our tea, young lady.' After an afternoon of rick sliding, horse riding and cowslip gathering, aunt Kate, with a clean blouse and apron, prepared jam sandwiches, huge slices of fruit cake, and big jugs of hot tea. Rene and I and some of the farm children carried the tea to the men, who left their steaming, snorting and slavering horses, now lifting great hooves, to crash them back to earth, as their tails twitched and slashed at the flies that tormented the wild eyed beasts, setting their harnesses jingling and clanging. I was allowed to put a little sugar on my hand, and offer it to them before starting my own tea.

'There's going to be a good harvest this year, Kate,' says George, 'but it won't make no difference to the working man, he won't get no more, 'deed he won't. I tell you, it's enough to turn a man into a Bolshie.' Then aunt Kate said 'He ought to be in Parliament, Alice, and I wish he would go for good.'

As soon as the last crust had been eaten, and foreheads and moustaches wiped with red spotted handkerchiefs, it was time to start again.

'Huppa! Huppa!' said uncle George, as with a great surge of movement the stamping, restless horses, flicking their saliva like foam, moved off with the men. 'See you at supper, Alice. You won't be gone, will you?' 'Oh I dare say,' gran called back. 'Well, Pearl, we'd better be making tracks . . . Help your aunt Kate with the tea things, and we'll be on our way'. 'You can't go home without any flowers for your mum, now, can you? Our Rene will show you. Don't pick too many from one plant,' said aunt Kate. My heart sank when I saw what we had to carry home. Nevertheless, I was pronounced a strong willing child.

Back now, along a shadowy road, the setting sun firing the church windows. One last jump on the gravestones. 'After all, they've been dead a long time, gran!' 'Pearl, if you do that again your name will go down in the

Black Book. If it thunders tonight, God is very angry with you.' She meant it.
'Gran,' I said thinking that if I talked she wouldn't walk so fast: 'Do you think it's wicked to talk to a boy?'
'Wicked?' gran replied (a past master in evasion) 'I don't see as it's wicked, but you don't want to have anything to do with *them* yet.'
'Do you still love grandad, gran?' 'I dare say. Now that's enough questions for a little girl today.'

There was no stopping for lemonade in a public house for gran, so I thought it would be better if I kept quiet and walked quickly, for grandad would be home for his tea, and Uncle Wally would be there too. So the rest of the journey was done in silence, punctuated now and then with 'Well, I never!' or, 'I dare say', or, 'No! little miss previous.'

I often wondered where her thoughts really were. Maybe she was back to the time when she walked for miles, finding the best primroses, only to give them to whoever wanted them. 'I hope my fire isn't out, young Pearl, your uncle gets so cross!' He was twenty and very patronising to me!

When we finally opened the door of 61 High Street, Wally was sitting in the kitchen chair and the fire was out! 'Pearl,' he said, 'I'm going to my room to work (He was a clerk in Chichester). Bring me some tea, and be quick about it.'

After taking his tea up I shouted, 'What did your last servant die of?'
'Oh, go and eat coke', he replied irritably.
'Stuff cake up your jumper'.
I kissed gran and grandad and went back to 28 Broyle Road, greeting mum and dad with 'I've had a lovely time; shall I have a boy friend one day?'
'I hope so,' said dad 'I shan't be able to keep you forever, I expect some muggins will come along!'

THE APPLE PICKERS

'Queenie,'
'Yes,'
'What shall we do?'
'How about bringing your worm hospital down to my garden?'
'My mum won't let me, she says it drops straw everywhere.'
'Can you put your rabbits into the doll's pram?'
'No My mum says no to everything, does yours?'
'Everything! I think when they go to tea with each other, they say "we'll just say no to everything"'
'All this going to tea, if they're not saying something about some old film, they're trying to stop us doing some good works. Look at the fuss they made when we just let the chickens out so they could have a walk. I can't see them shut up in some old chicken house.'
'Well, what shall we do then?'
'I'm still going to do good works.'
'Have you seen old Bushie's apple tree?'
'Yes, but the apples are still green and like marbles. Who wants *them*?'
'I know she's old. I expect she would like someone to pick her apples.'
'Yes, she doesn't want to break her old leg climbing up a ladder, does she?'
'I think she would be jolly grateful.'
'Then we could sell them for her!'

'Let's go and look at the tree and shake it a bit.'

'I'll bite this one, They're very hard.'

'Ugh! Still some people like them when they're sharp. My mum says she *loves* a sharp apple.'

'I'll stand on the box, you give me that thick stick there, - no that one, its only holding up an old window in the greenhouse.'

'Oh! blow. Now the window's smashed, look at the glass, it couldn't have been very good.'

'Suppose old Bushie comes out now.'

'She won't mind, she'll thank us for picking the apples. She might pay us, then we can knock everyone's trees around here and we won't have time to go to school. Now hold the box and I'll bang the branches with this stick, I'm going to get down now because my arms are tired. You get up . . . *Harder than that Queenie.*'

'My arms are aching, I want to get down.'

'Alright then, I think we have knocked down enough. I think she will be ever so pleased, nearly all the apples are on the ground now.'

'They're a bit bruised and some of them are broken.'

'Well they won't have to be cut up will they?'

'I know my mum always says "Now I have to cut up the apples", so I'm sure she will be pleased.'

'Oh!, crumbs, old Bushie's coming out of her door.'

'She's waving her stick.'

'Hello Bushie, look what we've done for you!'

'I don't think she's very pleased.'

'Look, there's *MY* mum and *YOUR* mum.'

'What are they shouting for?'

'Ooh! Aah! That hurt mum, why don't you all stop shouting? My head aches. Gran says you mustn't slap me because your wedding ring hurts my little head, Oohh! Mum!

Bye Queenie'

EMM AND EMPIRE DAY

Empire Day was in May and was celebrated in Priory Park for all who wanted to go. It was compulsory for the local schools unless you were lucky enough to catch a summer cold. I hated this day and always thought I would faint because we had to stand in the heat and listen to the mayoral speech which none of us could hear or understand.

After that was finished came "Nymphs and Shepherds" sung by at least four schools, all out of time, but when it was over we had the afternoon off. On one particular occasion my mother met me in the park and told me we were going to aunt Emm's for tea. I was quite pleased about this, for to see my mothers ire and the effrontery of Emm who always had everything better than everyone else gave me a great deal of pleasure. I used to sit entranced while Beat, Emm's timid sister, interjected every time Emm started with 'Yes Emm, you did Emm. I'm sure Emm's right Lily.' 'Cheek!' said my mum later.

At four o'clock we arrived at 43 Grove Road where aunt Emm, freshly changed, with rouged cheeks and sausage curls peeping out from under a hairnet, waited with shaded eyes at her gate.

'Ugh!' said mum 'I shall be glad when this afternoon is over, I hope your dad won't be late calling for us.' 'Hello Lily, hello duck' said Emm, 'Tea's already laid and the kettle boiling. No one has to wait here.' 'Beat' she hollered into the open door of the kitchen, 'Turn the gas down, I want to show Lily my wallflowers. A gentleman stopped the other day and said he had never seen such wallflowers in his life and asked me whom he was addressing.'

'Mrs Earwaker sir,' 'Mrs *Erica*,' he said; 'So Lily, I'm going to ask my Henry if he would agree to change it. My Henry denies me nothing as you well know' said Emm, rearranging her curlers. Yes my mother did know, and she also knew, as Emm did, that no one could do anything with my dad that he didn't want to do. 'Just give her a week with Fred and she would soon change him!' When mum related this to him, he looked steadily at her and said, 'I'd like to see her try, my girl, I'd just like to see her try!'

From the garden we stepped into the little kitchen. 'My Henry's just washed all the walls Lily; hasn't he done well?' Mum gave a smothered sound of approval. 'Look Lily, my cupboard's painted inside and out.' With this she shut the doors with a bang. 'Have you ever seen a gas cooker like that or an oven so clean?' She opened the oven door and we all peered inside at nothing, while she ran her finger along the trift. 'My hubby cleans it. He would never allow *me* to, would he Beat?' 'No Emm' said Beat.

Decorated paper, cut into points, lined the shelves on which were shining saucepans. A knitted cotton dishcloth hung on the side of the limestone sink and the tap shone like gold. 'I'm just going to make the tea Lily' said Emm as she took down the tea caddy, the pattern now obliterated by a thumb and finger mark. One spoon for each of us and one for the pot. 'There,' she said, as she poured the boiling water onto the fragrant smelling tea, 'Ninepence a quarter from the Inter. None of your fourpenny stuff for me!'

We followed Emm and the teapot into the living room.

The table was laid like an altar with lace table-cloth, best china and knives from a mauve velvet-lined box. There were pink overlapping slices of ham from the "Inter", best butter from Liptons and rhubarb jam that no one could make like Emm. A large yellow sponge cake full of baking powder to make it rise high stood on a glass cake stand, and a junket too salt to eat because of an overdose of rennet. We dare not refuse any of it. I could not look at my mother who was trying to eat a truly rocklike cake.

When tea was over, we were taken upstairs to see Emm's new bedspread. It was mauve and made of shot silk, which was very fashionable at that time. On the floor as in everyone's bedroom then, red patterned linoleum, highly polished with small oval rush mats on top. Sideways across a corner stood a wash hand stand and basin and small towels, ready I suspected, for the doctor, in case of illness.

Hanging on the stair-rope we went down the narrow carpeted stairs and stood in hushed silence as we surveyed the sitting room. Curtains were drawn across the front window to protect the small rug from the light of the sun.

'I'll pull the curtains Lily' said Emm, pushing forward and hurling them back. 'There, ' she said 'Now we can see better.' Red wax tulips flowered everlastingly in Woolworths vases and little knick-knacks were placed at angles on every polished surface. A plaster paper fan disguised a perfectly honest little black grate, while fire tongs and poker leaned with studied perfection on the shining brass fender. Nothing here would be disturbed until Christmas Day.

A quick look at the well-known photographs we had seen everytime we had come: Emm and Henry in the garden, Beat at Bognor with a donkey; aunt Nell sitting in a deckchair with a black hat and a fur coat; groups of wedding parties staring with transfixed eyes at the camera. When we had left the shrine, as dad aptly called it, Emm gave one more glance at her spotless little room, the pride of her life. It was just the same for my mother in our home and they competed with each other constantly about what they had added to the house since they had last met, scrimping and saving from their meagre house-keeping money to keep their homes looking like little palaces.

'Well Emm, we shall have to be off' said my mother, (dad waited down the road, for he would never come to Emm's) 'Why don't you come to a concert at the Wesleyan Chapel, Lily?' said Emm. 'Beat and I are dancing in the chorus, dressed as men. Talk about a laugh, flannel trousers and high heeled shoes!' Mum was not amused! I'll come aunty Emm,' I said, 'All right Pearly, now here comes my hubby from work and he will want a cup of tea won't you lovey?' Hubby was a tall handsome man who used to put his hand around the back of my neck and remark that it was like a *sparrow's*.

'Goodbye Emm and Beat, goodbye Henry,' (What made him marry Emm?) 'Goodbye Lil and Pearlie, love to Fred' I always blushed when she said this for I knew dad was skulking in the doorway of the Kingsham Road Co-op.

Once on the road home Mum let rip. 'I don't know why I go down there. Fancy those two women dancing in the chorus at their age.' A little dancing in the chorus, I thought, wouldn't have done my mum any harm!

By now we had reached the Co-op doorway and there dad stood, grim-faced at the prospect of being late for the "Star" and his game of cribbage. 'Carry the rhubarb Fred' demanded my mother. 'I can't believe it,' he exploded, 'we've got masses in the garden.' 'Yes,' said mum, 'but how can you say no to Emm?' 'I could very easily, very easily indeed' replied dad 'and I hope you haven't invited her to tea, because I shall be out.' 'Rude man,' replied my mum walking quickly ahead.

Oh! lucky lucky Emm, I thought, that you found Henry. What a good job it wasn't Fred.

SHERBERT

exploded, 'we've got masses in the garden.' 'Yes,' said mum, 'but how can

'Queenie'

'Yes'

'My mum and dad and your mum and dad and all the others are going up to the Star tonight'.

'Yes, that's why I have this lace dress on.'

'I've got mine on too, my best shoes pinch me and I had curlers put in my hair last night, did you?'

'No, because mine is natural.'

'That's a fib, it's not.'

'Well it is a little bit.'

'Anyway you've got a black mark on your dress.'

'If I spit on my finger and rub it, it will soon come off.'

'Now it's bigger.'

'Let's go into grans now and wait for the others. Hello gran, have you got any sherbert?'

'You always want something Pearl. What have you done to your dress? Just wait until your mum sees it; she'll never take you to the Star like that.'

'Good, we don't want to go anyway, do we Queenie?'

'No we don't'

'I just want to go into the garden and scratch the pig's back with a stick and let the chickens out, do you?'

'Yes, if I make my dress dirty too they won't take us to the Star.'

'Let's go into the garden and I'll put dirt on your dress — there, shall I put some on your socks?'

'Look at my leg where my mum smacked me. Didn't they look cross shouting and slapping us?'

'I don't care, they've gone now and we can do what we like.'

'They told us to sit in the kitchen and draw.'

'I know. They always say - "Do some drawing." They say that when they can't think of anything else.'

'Do you want some more sherbert Queenie?'

'Yes, but where does gran keep it?'

'In this cupboard.'

'It doesn't say sherbert on it.'

'Of course it doesn't silly! They put sherbert on the box, not on every packet and I expect gran has thrown it away. Get some water and I'll make you some.'

'Why doesn't it fizz?'

'I expect the packet's damp.'

'Tastes awful. I think I'm going to be sick.'

'Don't spit it out. I'll stir it: go on, have another drink.'

'Oh,' 'Hello mum and dad, I'm just making Queenie some sherbert'. OOH! you've slapped my other leg and it's all red. I was only being helpful.'

'Why are you making Queenie drink salt and water?'

'I'm going to tell my other gran what you've done.'

How was I to know it was the canker powder for the dogs ears? Whatever you do nobody is ever grateful. I expect when I get home my mum will put on that old record about some boy who had no mother and father. I wonder what he did.

MORE EMM AND BEAT

I lived with my parents in a red brick cottage, No.28 Broyle Road. The cleaning of it was my mother's passion, and woe betide anyone calling before the 'brights' were done or the linoleum polished. The house was fragrant with lavender polish and brasso, the steps snowy white and the lace curtains stiff with starch.

Monday mornings were special. This was washing day so the clothes had to be boiled in the big stone copper, then put out on the line before any of her neighbours. It was also on Monday mornings that her two cousins Emm and Beat would be most likely to call. This infuriated my mother. 'Just do it to catch me out,' she would say.

Sharp at ten o'clock there came the dreaded call. 'Yoo-hoo Lily.' Done up to the nines and reeking of Californian Poppy as my mother once told my aunt Ethel.

Emm had married. Beat had not, but lived with Emm. 'Hunting in pairs.' my father drily remarked.

'Come on Lily, put the kettle on. My washing has been out since seven o'clock.'

A flush rose in my mother's cheeks and neck and she banged the cups and saucers down; meanwhile the two women taking off their coats and hats and fluffing out their tonged hair, crossing their large, silk-clad legs, prepared to enjoy my mother's annoyance. I loved the slight rasp of silk as they did so. Then taking out their scented cigarettes, they lit up and puffed away, to my utter delight.

'I made a beautiful sponge Lily,' said Emm, turning to her sister, 'didn't I Beat?'
Beat always agreed with Emm, nodding her head at every question.
'Come up high didn't it Beat?'
'Oh yes, Emm. Yes it did.'

They were always telling tales of their past jobs. 'Oh, tell me more' I said hopping from one leg to the other, my mouth bulging with sweets, as they burst into peals of laughter. My mother remained stony-faced.

When they had drunk their tea they went into the garden, commenting on how slow all the plants were compared to Emm's garden. Back in the kitchen my mother lifted the steaming clothes from the copper with a rolling pin and hurled them into the sink. 'Perhaps that will send them off,' she muttered, as we all peered at each other through the clouds of steam.

'Can't stay any longer Lily', said Emm. 'My hair's a ruin and I'm going to a social.' My mother smiled. 'Goodbye Pearl, my duck, - not very tall is she, Lil? and what a lot of hair she has on her legs and arms. Good job she's fair.' After a quick strum on the piano she finally reached the door. 'Just off to see Ethel, Lil. Pearlie, you must come and have one of *my* teas.'
'Ugh!' said my mother when they had gone. 'That Emm and Beat.'
But I looked forward to the next Monday.

DINNER AT GRAN'S

Ever since I started school I had always gone to my grandmother's for dinner. I had spent so much time with her as a small child that I knew she would miss me and so it was she who always met me at the school gate at twelve-o-clock instead of going through the town to my own home.

I was taken along the Cherry Orchard, a little lane running around the back of the school which led into Parchment Street, and then on to 61 High Street where my dinner was always in the oven.

On Mondays a cousin took me home because auntie Doris came with her two children and did her washing with gran. I remember on one occasion both women up to their pink elbows in soap suds and seeing me standing at the wash house door wrung out a large sheet, smoothed their hair back and wiped dry their hands, showing me the wrinkled skin, saying, 'don't ever get married Pearl'. Hmm, I thought, I'll get married but I won't do the washing.

Monday's dinner was always the same as were the other days of the week, and had been since my mother was a little girl. Cold beef, warmed up roast potatoes and sprouts, with jelly and custard to follow. Next day we had stew made from the remains of the joint with dumplings like bullets! I used to slosh vinegar all over the stew so that at least it tasted of something, while gran looked offended.

She never said much to me but ate her meal very fast, her eyes moving all the while, then folded her hands in her lap and looked out at the apple tree in the garden until I had eaten my meal. I talked a lot to her but her only answers were 'well I never' or' I dare say', and 'oh! Pearl how you do talk'.

Once when a little cousin came to dinner gran enquired whether she learned about Jesus, 'Yes I do', said the little girl, 'but I expect he is only made of china'. Gran looked at her for a long time and I am sure I saw the faintest of smiles on those prim lips.

On Wednesdays my favourite dinner of the week was steak and kidney pie made with a suet crust. We never had a sweet except on Mondays. On cold days I was allowed to sit with my feet on the fender in front of a large coal fire which filled the room with warmth and smoke, and I ate my dinner from a tray.

Sometimes grandad came home to his dinner before I went back to school and we all sat down to liver and crow with brown gravy. Grandad had a large moustache and ate with a two-pronged fork and a knife with yellow bone handles. When he had finished eating he wiped his mouth with a red spotted handkerchief and usually said the same thing to me; 'how are you getting on at school then, my duck? You'll have to do as well as your gran, she reads the whole of the "News of the World" out loud to me on Sundays.' I wondered if that was what you had to do if you got married.

On Fridays I nursed the thought of Shippams sausages bursting with pork and sage, served with mashed potatoes and a dollop of Daddie's sauce. For more that fifty years these meals were never varied and they remained so until I left school and went to work. All my little cousins at one time or another went there to dinner too, and the meals never changed for them either.

On Fridays, years later, I used to visit gran to chat about old times, but her greatest pleasure was when my husband painted a life-size portrait of her sitting in her big winged arm chair. As tradesfolk came to the door they were called in to see her "photograph", as she called it. We still have that picture.

On her eighty-ninth birthday I had just had a cup of tea with her when she said; 'Tell your mother Pearl, I think I had better come and live with her and your dad. Run along now, and see what they say', I was forty years old at the time. And so she did, until she died aged ninety two, just after talking to me about her garden and the apple tree which she said bore the sweetest apples she had ever eaten.

It was a nice thought to die with.

THE WALK

We come to the end of the Sunday night walk and the sun is leaving a golden sky. We can still see our way down the rutted chalky lane and I can smell the bruised green almond scent of the cow parsley and the bitter red-veined dock. Dark fields stretch out, cream studded with mushrooms.

The fruit of the deadly night-shade hangs heavy and enticing. I close my hand around the silky berries and my father shouts a warning. I look for my mother who is loitering in the pearly dark. She never can keep up.

My father calls 'Lily, Lily. We'll never get to the Star!' I look up to the sky, 'Which star, dad? which star?'

DOWN TOWN

Soon after my aunt's wedding, mum, dad and brother Len moved to Franklin Place, a pleasant terrace of Victorian houses, at one time occupied by the tradesfolk of Chichester. They had three bedrooms and three downstairs rooms, which included a stone-flagged kitchen. There was a pleasant little garden, and the Roman wall covered in sweet betsy towered over it. Priory Park lay on the other side. This house was my mother's pride and joy. Never was there one so clean, with crisp curtains, sparkling windows and polished linoleum. As we came home from school mum was waiting with a mop to rub over the passage where our sandals had been!

On Saturdays my mother and aunt would go shopping in the town, where the gentle flow of traffic bothered no-one. Geerings and Denyers flourished as drapers, and there were always cottons, a piece of material for cushion covers, or a pattern for my summer dress with knickers to match, which my aunt made — same pattern every year! The method of paying was worth recalling: an assistant put the bill and money in a wooden ball, which she screwed up tight. She then put this into what appeared to be a mechanical nest, pulled a chain and the ball went whizzing to the cashier who sat, so it seemed, near the ceiling. She then sent back the change by the same route.

The next visit would be to the Butter Market, and a nice kipper or herrings for dad's Saturday tea. After that my mother and aunt would go to Mr Denyer the draper, who sold stockings and corsets and underclothes. As soon as one entered the door he would loudly call: 'Ladies' vests this way please. Knickers, fleecy-lined, this counter, madam.'

Mum would go very red. 'As if you want everyone to know, Ethel!'

Finally there were tea and cakes in the Cathedral tea rooms above Lennards, the shoe shop. One pot of tea for three, one shilling; cakes fourpence, scones tuppence. Woolworths had not arrived then, but Bull's hardware, Bastows the chemist, Austins the wool shop, flourished. Everyone seemed to ride bicycles, and these were propped up against the kerb, making it difficult to find an opening to cross the road. West Street always seemed to be flooded with sunshine and I remember the tall railings enclosing the Cathedral.

On Saturday nights we went to the Picturedrome, where lurid posters, recently pasted and full of wrinkles, informed you that Billie Dove was in a film called 'Bad To The Bone'. After sobbing our way through the drama, a 3d. piece of fish and a pennyworth of chips, bought from Carpenters at Northgate, consoled us.

What a perfect country market city Chichester was. Every Georgian house had a lovely garden. Allotments flanked one side of the city. Sunday evening in the Park was band night, and you stood in your best clothes next to your parents making eyes at the boys. (I thought I was beginning to get the hang of it!) Then there was the Tin Lizzie which clanked and rattled to Selsey for sixpence. Selsey was just a village with a seaside and deserted beaches, Bognor still a paradise for local families and Sunday School outings, the sand deep and golden.

'Who's for a trip in the Skylark?'
I was always for a trip in the Skylark!

It will never be the same for us . . . but I have only to close my eyes and I can sit in the meadows of Fordwater while my mother cuts sandwiches and my father makes a bullrush bouquet or go cockling at Dell Quay, rabbiting in the Wellington fields, or singing like angels with the rest of the girls' choir in St Peter the Less.